C000122268

DONALD,
HIS FRIENDS
and
NEW
ORLEANS
PIRATES

PALMETTO
PUBLISHING
Charleston, SC
www.PalmettoPublishing.com

Copyright © 2024 by Carl DeWing

All rights reserved.
This book or any portion thereof may not be reproduced or used in any
manner whatsoever without the express written permission of the publisher
except for the use of brief quotations in a book review.

Hardcover ISBN: 979-8-8229-4444-2
Paperback ISBN: 979-8-8229-4445-9
eBook ISBN: 979-8-8229-4446-6

Carl DeWing

DONALD, HIS FRIENDS
and
NEW ORLEANS PIRATES

CONTENTS

CHAPTER ONE

"I hate that governor," exclaimed Jean Lafitte, who was anxiously looking through the wrong side of jail bars. He paced the jail cell in frustration. There wasn't much room to pace with many of his men in the tiny cell with him.

Governor Claiborne of Louisiana had seen to it to have Lafitte and his men arrested for buying and selling goods that pirates had sold to Lafitte.

"He's not only hurting us, but he'll be putting a number of local stores out of business. Somebody ought to shoot the bastard," said Lafitte.

He glanced out the tiny jail window to what little he could see of New Orleans. "We've got to get rid of this governor or he's going to ruin everything. I don't have the political clout to do that, but I have friends in high places who maybe can do something about him."

"So what do we do now?" asked Lafitte's brother Pierre, who shivered from the cold that was creeping up his feet from the concrete floor. "Do we sit here and rot in jail until they find us guilty and hang us as pirates?"

"Nah," said Lafitte. "I have a very good friend in New Orleans who's an attorney. He'll bail us out, and we'll get out of town before the governor realizes we're gone."

Within hours, Lafitte got word to Jim Marshall, a local attorney and a good friend. When Marshall showed up to post bail, he gently gave Lafitte a ribbing for causing the governor to throw him and his men in jail. "Maybe if you donated to the governor's reelection campaign you would stay out of jail," said a smiling Marshall.

Nevertheless, Marshall was happy to help his friend get out of jail, and within hours Lafitte, his brother, and most of his men were on their way to his headquarters on Barataria, an island in the Mississippi Delta, about forty miles south of New Orleans.

Most of the merchants he sold to were happy to hear Lafitte was out of jail. That meant they would continue to receive merchandise at half the price they would have to pay if they bought stuff from New York and the East Coast.

When he dealt with merchants in New Orleans, he was soft-spoken and very polite. He spoke with a slight French accent and was genuinely liked by all who did business with him.

The appearance of Lafitte was that of a gentleman. Unlike most of his men who wore regular clothes, Lafitte wore tailored suits and a broad-brimmed hat.

CHAPTER TWO

There was another side of Jean Lafitte. He was also a man who was not afraid to shoot someone. In fact, the week before he went to New Orleans and wound up in jail, Lafitte killed a man in a duel who had challenged him to be the leader of Barataria. Had authorities known about the killing, he might not have been let out of jail and been a serious candidate for hanging.

The man Lafitte killed was a rough-looking individual called Raoul who had left a pirate ship to join those working for Lafitte. Raoul was a stocky man with a beard and long scraggly hair along with a mean personality. He was given the task of unloading the goods from the pirate ships and taking it to the warehouse on Barataria Island where it was stacked to be later taken to New Orleans to be sold. After a week of this, he decided this was enough. Raoul could run the island better than Lafitte.

So on a day when Lafitte returned to the island, Raoul confronted him and, with his hand on a pistol tucked in his belt, said in a very haughty tone, "Monsieur Lafitte. I think your time on the island is done. I think you should return to New Orleans and find another business."

"Oh!?" said a surprised Lafitte. "And who all would run the island once I'm gone?"

By this time a small crowd saw the confrontation and had gathered around to watch. Raoul began to notice this and was reluctant to pull the pistol for fear that some of the men loyal to Lafitte might intervene. Nevertheless, Raoul summed up his courage and said, "I will. I can run this island better than you."

"Oh," said Lafitte, noticing the growing support by the gathering crowd.

"Let's settle this in a civilized way. Since we both strongly disagree on who should be in charge, I challenge you to a duel. If you win, you will be in charge. If I win, you will be dead."

Raoul hesitated for a moment, realizing he was outnumbered by the gathering crowd, and decided this might be the best way to go. He was a good shot with a pistol, and the chance of running an operation that brought in about ten thousand dollars a month, which in that day and age, was more than he could pass up. Besides, how good could this fancy-dressed dude be in a duel. "I accept," declared Raoul.

A cheer went up from the crowd. "Then, tomorrow at noon, in front of the warehouse," said Lafitte.

The next day, when the time came for the duel, Lafitte's brother Pierre ran the contest. "Each of you will start back-to-back, and when I start counting, you will take ten steps out, turn, and fire. If either of you turn and fire before finishing the ten steps, the men on the sidelines will shoot the violator," said Pierre.

He then started to count down the steps. "…seven, eight, nine, ten." Lafitte wheeled around in a split second, aimed, and fired just as Raoul was aiming his pistol. Lafitte's bullet hit Raoul in the chest, causing him to stumble backward just as Raoul pulled the trigger, sending his bullet above Lafitte's head. He then collapsed on his back. Raoul took two deep breaths, and then died.

Had he known that Lafitte was as good with a pistol as anyone, he might have backed out and left Barataria a chastised but alive man.

Lafitte turned to the men watching the spectacle and, with the pistol still smoking and pointing up, asked, "Anyone else want to run this island?" Dead silence followed. "Then get back to work."

But war storm clouds were gathering. This was 1814. The British, who had invaded the northeast United States in 1812, had decided to go south, then up the Mississippi River and invade from the west. New Orleans was only a temporary problem for the invading army.

Little did he know, Lafitte was about to be thrust into a war that would change his life, and the life of all the citizens of New Orleans, forever.

CHAPTER THREE

On the edge of town in a meadow near a dark, shaded area where the trees grew close together, an almost eighteen-year-old Donald walked with his two friends, Julianne and Ramon. Donald was the accepted leader of this small group of teenagers. And he valued their trust and friendship. Handsome for his age, he had curly blond hair and a slim physique.

Suddenly, Donald stopped short. The teenagers could see a group of men passing by on a little-used dirt road on the edge of the meadow. Some of the men were carrying large bags, and one was pushing a wheelbarrow covered by a canvas tarp.

Julianne, who preferred to be called Julie, pulled her light winter jacket on tighter, and asked, "Who are those men?"

"They belong to Jean Lafitte, the pirate," said Ramon. "My father does a lot of work in his blacksmith shop for Lafitte and his men, and most of them are not nice."

"Lafitte's not a pirate," said Donald emphatically. "My father buys a lot of stuff from him that we sell in our store. He's a privateer. He buys goods from sailing vessels."

"Yeah," said Ramon with a sense of sarcasm. "But Lafitte's buying stolen goods from pirates. My father told me Lafitte and his brother, Pierre, and about a dozen of his men had recently been arrested by the local army. They were attempting to smuggle about four thousand dollars' worth of pirate merchandise into New Orleans."

"That doesn't mean he's a pirate," said Donald. "He's just selling goods he's got from ships that come to his headquarters down south."

"Lafitte receives goods from pirates who plunder ships in the Gulf of Mexico," said Ramon, his voice rising.

"Maybe some of the stuff comes from pirates, but why just throw the goods away? Somebody ought to get some use out of it," said Donald in an irritating tone. "Besides, the people of New Orleans get to buy stuff a lot cheaper than if it came from New York."

"What?" said Ramon, his eyebrows going up with an incredulous look. "They're bad people. Some of the people they stole from may have been killed."

The two young men were now nose to nose.

"Hey, you guys, they're not bothering us," Julie said with mock indignation. "Stop arguing! I'm leaving," she said emphatically.

And with that, she turned and ran off in the direction of her house, holding her long dress up a little so she wouldn't stumble, with her long blond hair bouncing as she ran.

The two boys at first were stunned, watching her run off like that. "See what you did," said Donald.

"What I did?" responded Ramon. "I'm only telling you what I know about Lafitte and his men."

As Julie was running toward her home, she thought maybe she had overreacted. But she was done with hearing them argue.

CHAPTER FOUR

Julie had just finished fixing dinner when her father, Dr. Bernard Finch, walked into the house just after sunset. She worried about him working so hard, being one of the few doctors in the area.

Julie saw her father had a serious look on his face and asked, "What's wrong?"

"Julie," he said. "The town has received some bad news. The British fleet has arrived just outside of Lake Borgne and are believed to be headed this way. If they reach New Orleans, they will devastate the town, and you will be in danger."

Julie was startled by her father's stern message. "What do you mean I'll be in danger?" asked Julie. "Won't we all be in danger?"

Although she also knew what he wasn't saying. It was rarely spoken around women and children, but she had heard the stories.

When the British invaded Hampton, New Jersey, and other eastern communities in the beginning of the War of 1812, they not only pillaged the communities of anything of value, they also raped many women.

Her father decided he didn't want to alarm his daughter any more than he already had, so he didn't include the part about the British soldiers pillaging the East Coast towns.

During dinner, the two were silent, deep in thought about what the future might bring. Then, her father spoke up. "I think if the British do come to New Orleans, we should leave town. We should take some of the back roads going east to avoid any contact with the redcoats. I'm not saying we will, but if we do I want you to be ready. Maybe pack a few clothes and other things if that's what we decide to do."

"OK," said Julie in a downcast way. She was a very smart young lady and knew what might happen should the British be successful at invading New Orleans.

After dinner, Julie went to bed that night but had a hard time sleeping, thinking about the possible danger the city faced and how she and her father might survive a British attack.

CHAPTER FIVE

The next morning, Donald made it to class and sat between Julie and Ramon. The teacher announced, "We're going to take a walk to the town square to see a very special person. His name is General Andrew Jackson. He is coming to town because there are rumors the British army and navy might invade the region."

Donald stood up from his desk and confirmed what the teacher had said.

"My father has been following the war in the East and said there was always a chance the British might come this way."

"That's right," said the teacher. "So we need to know what the general will do to protect us."

As the students walked toward the town square, Ramon stuck his hands in his pockets and shook his head. "It's 1814 and the English are still fighting us. Why can't they just leave us alone?"

There had been fears the British might come to the Gulf Coast and invade America from the South. That they might also plunder the South was of grave concern now to many residents of New Orleans.

That Monday morning, General Andrew Jackson arrived in New Orleans in a carriage and was greeted by a large crowd who was anxious to hear what he had to say.

Donald, Julie, and Ramon and the rest of the students, along with many New Orleans citizens, gathered in the square as the general spoke from the balcony of his headquarters on Royal Street. They heard Jackson declare that he had come to protect the city, that he would "drive the British into the sea or perish in the effort."

To their surprise, both Donald and Julie saw their fathers in the front of the crowd. Ramon's father was not present.

The general's speech confirmed to Julie there was a chance the war might be coming to New Orleans and sent shivers down her spine.

The boys were excited. Here was a chance to be a part of a defense of the city. Although Donald and Ramon had no military experience, they had done a lot of hunting of rabbits and squirrels. They had become really good marksmen for their age. But killing a human was totally foreign to them.

"Hey," said Donald. "We should join General Jackson's army. You think our fathers would let us do that?"

"I don't see why not," responded Ramon. "We know how to shoot. We're as good a shot as a lot of men in town."

That bothered Julie. "You're not seriously thinking of doing that?" she asked. She liked the two boys and worried about the possibility they may have to go to war.

Julie also really began to understand the danger the city was possibly facing. Donald and Ramon might be hurt or killed should the fighting come to New Orleans. And for the first time, she realized how much affection she had for the two. They were close friends, and she worried for their safety.

CHAPTER SIX

After school, Ramon went back to the blacksmith shop to help his dad. Donald and Julie lingered for a while talking about what the general said and worrying about a possible invasion.

She suddenly had this urge to give Donald a big hug of affection. He was surprised by the sudden display of emotion. But he instinctively put his arms around her. For the first time, he felt a passion with her he had never felt before. For a moment they held each other. When they parted, they both felt a little embarrassed by the affection they had never exhibited before.

"What was that about?" Donald asked smiling.

"I worry that if the British did come, you and Ramon might be killed," she said, choking back a tear.

"Nah," said Donald. "Why would they come to New Orleans? But if they do, I plan to do my part." He felt even more determined to show what he was made of. "I hope to volunteer with my dad if he'll let me. I'll help defend the city should the Brits show up."

But a few days later, the British did show up. A number of ships had anchored off shore in the Gulf of Mexico just outside of Lake Borgne, about sixty miles southeast of New Orleans.

Because the lake was shallow in places, the British advanced in small boats to the other side of the lake, then marched several miles through a swampy area to a place about seven miles southeast of New Orleans. There they established a camp in a dry, open area between the swamp and the Mississippi River.

The first contingent to arrive was about two thousand men with several thousand more on the way. They expected little resistance from the Americans. Their leaders planned to invade New Orleans in the next day or so, and the troops would enjoy the spoils of war in many ways. They then would go up the Mississippi River and attack the US East Coast from the west.

CHAPTER SEVEN

In the meantime, General Jackson had pulled together several different groups of volunteers and army regulars, numbering about four thousand plus men to face the British. The biggest number were the Tennessean volunteers, most of which were rough, tough, buckskin- or homespun-clad, and generally were wild and murderous-looking backwoodsmen, many wearing coonskin caps. There were also a large group of men from Arkansas, a local regular army unit, almost one hundred Choctaw Indians, and others who joined Jackson's army.

Donald and his father joined a battalion of local businessmen, lawyers, plantation owners, and their sons, which numbered about 280 men. Their battalion leader was a man named Captain Thomas Beale. He was a local businessman but had some military experience and had the confidence and demeanor of a leader who could bring the men together into an organized fighting force.

During a formation of the local group, Beale warned the men about the danger of fighting the British. "Some of you might get killed or injured," he said. But he emphasized, "It's important to defend the city. Be aware of the danger to your wives, sons, and daughters."

Beale finished his speech with a resounding, "Are you ready for this fight?"

To a man, the shout went up. "Yes, yes yes…" This included Donald and his father as the men swore to defend the city to the best of their ability.

Donald began to realize this battle might be dangerous, and lives could be lost.

After the meeting, Donald turned to his father. "Thank you for all you have done for me. I plan on coming out of this alive, but if I don't, I appreciate being your son."

"Son," his father said, "we're all coming out of this alive. We will save our city and our family."

Jackson was not sure how he could form such a diverse group of units into a cohesive fighting force. He assigned one of his lieutenants to try and bring the various groups together and to coordinate activities once the fighting did start.

CHAPTER EIGHT

Meanwhile, Jean Lafitte and his brother Pierre had earlier returned to their hideout in the Delta south of New Orleans. They had bailed out of jail with the help of his attorney and some of his local friends and were subsequently pardoned by a local judge.

It was at Barataria that a British ship sailed to the island, and under a white flag of truce indicated that some officers wanted to talk to Lafitte. He didn't like the English. He knew about the devastation they had caused on the East Coast. In fact, he disliked the British as much as the Italians and French.

He was also concerned the British might destroy New Orleans and ruin his entire business enterprise. But he very politely invited a small contingent of British officers to come ashore to find out what they were about.

After cordial introductions, Lafitte welcomed the officers. "I welcome you as friends, and may we depart as friends." He then gave them a sumptuous dinner and an after-dinner wine.

It was then the British officers offered him a thirty-thousand-pound bribe if he and his men helped with the invasion of New Orleans. Lafitte was noncommittal and said he would have to think about it.

"I need to think how many men I might lose and whether my operation might be endangered. Please give me some time to think about this, and I'll let you know."

Lafitte liked the thought of getting a bribe of that much money. But, in the long run, he could make twice or maybe three times that amount by doing business in New Orleans without the British.

After the British left, Lafitte sent a message to Governor Claiborne, warning what the British were planning. But the governor hated Lafitte, still considering him a pirate and ignored his warnings.

Later, Lafitte slipped into New Orleans undetected to meet with General Jackson. At the meeting, Jackson was surprised by the nice clothes Lafitte was wearing and his intelligent personality. Although Jackson at first was dubious of this man who some considered a pirate.

Lafitte told Jackson, "My men are expert gunners with cannons. Also, I have stored away huge amounts of gunpowder and flints while on Barataria, which I offer to you to defend New Orleans."

The general was impressed with the offer. Especially since Jackson's troops were short on munitions, the general's opinion of Lafitte began to change.

Lafitte's knowledge of the swamps and bayous and the surrounding terrain of New Orleans was an added reason for Jackson to accept Lafitte's help.

CHAPTER NINE

And what about Ramon and his dad? They joined the battalion of local men and over the next few days helped erect a ten-to-fifteen-foot-high barrier south of New Orleans to stop the advancing British. The mile-wide berm extended from the Mississippi River on the right to a swampy area on the left. Cannons were mounted on the top of the barrier aimed at an area to the south where the British had begun to set up an encampment.

Ramon worked hard in helping to erect the barrier. Jackson assigned him the task of getting the bags of gunpowder and cannon balls from a protected bunker and bringing them to Lafitte's men who would man the cannons.

Ramon also began to change his mind about Lafitte's men. He confessed to his father. "They are bad men," Ramon admitted. "Yes, they use bad language. Yes, most of them have criminal backgrounds. But they also are expected to work hard at loading and firing the cannons with accuracy when the fighting does start. In my contact with them, none have shown me any disrespect."

"Be careful, my son. Do not let their loose morals and past criminal behaviors change your ways," his father warned.

Ramon's father, as a blacksmith, was assigned to make repairs to any of the cannons or the rifles of the men protecting the rampart. Because he did a lot of work for Lafitte and his organization, he had firsthand knowledge about Lafitte's men.

CHAPTER TEN

Dr. Finch and his daughter, Julie, met with General Jackson and volunteered to treat anyone who was injured in the expected battle. At first, Jackson was skeptical of a sixty-year-old doctor being able to treat injured men. But Dr. Finch said he had considerable experience. "I was a very young doctor in the American Revolution and took care of many wounded soldiers. I have been practicing medicine all my adult life."

He did not include the worry in the back of his mind that if it looked like the British would be able to push past the defensive line and invade New Orleans, he and Julie would do their best to escape to the East.

"All right," said Jackson. "I will assign you to an abandoned plantation mansion just behind the line of defense to treat any injured men as soon as possible."

This was in the same mansion General Jackson had also taken over as his headquarters. From a second-floor window, using a telescope looking over the defensive rampart in front of him, he could see the British troops setting up a temporary camp far to the south.

Julie was asked to join dozens of other women in town making bandages and waiting for any injured men to be brought to a number of local sites that had been set up as temporary hospitals to treat casualties.

It was there that Julie met Donald's mother for the first time. Agatha Borden wasn't exactly friendly to this young girl. She had heard that Donald and Julie were meeting outside of the school hours in unaccompanied visits.

"So you are the young lady that's a friend of Donald," said Agatha.

"Yes ma'am," responded Julie.

"I hear you are meeting my son outside of school hours. Isn't that a little inappropriate for a young lady like yourself?" asked the older woman in a rather stern tone.

Julie began to realize this was not a friendly encounter and became very uncomfortable. "Well," she stammered, "we're just friends."

To which Agatha responded, "Perhaps you should spend more time with girls your age." With that, Agatha spun around and walked away.

Julie wasn't sure what to make of the encounter, turning with raised eyebrows to some girls who were with her and who giggled at the confrontation. But for the rest of the evening, she made sure she stayed away from Donald's mother while helping other women get ready for any injured men arriving from the battlefield.

CHAPTER ELEVEN

General Jackson had received word from a spy that the first contingent of British men established a camp about four miles down from where the Americans had their line of defense. But the British were not aware of any serious American military presence. They thought any defensive effort the Americans might come up with would be easily overcome on their way through New Orleans.

Jackson was determined to prove them wrong. He gathered his men and gave a rousing speech, not only to raise their spirits for the gathering conflict, but to outline how they intended to win the fight.

Jackson told the assembled men, "We're going to surprise the hell out of them. Tonight we will make an attack while the British are relaxing in their camp."

"I've also ordered a large schooner from New Orleans to quietly move down the Mississippi River adjacent to where the British are camped." The ship was mostly manned by Lafitte's Baratarian pirates, men who had the knowledge and experience to man the cannons onboard the craft.

It was just after dark that the craft was in place. Although some of the British soldiers noticed the ship above the levee several hundred yards to the left of them, they didn't think much of it, that it must be just a commercial vessel.

The scene was set for the first big battle to save New Orleans.

CHAPTER TWELVE

It was dark. The sun had set, and Donald and his father were back at the defensive line with the local militia and the other groups, including the Kentuckians, Tennesseans, and the Choctaw Indians. They were assigned to raid the unsuspecting British camp after sunset shortly after the ship opened fire from the river.

After forming up behind the rampart, they moved silently toward the British camp and anxiously awaited the signal from Lafitte's men on the schooner to charge the redcoats.

Donald was extremely nervous. He wasn't sure he could kill another human being. His father, noticing his son's apprehension, tried to calm his fears. "Son," he said, "this is going to be extremely dangerous. You either kill or be killed. These are wicked men who do not deserve to live."

This gave Donald the resolve he needed. "All right!" he said with conviction, trying to show his determination at doing what was necessary.

"You are here to protect your family, your friends, your city, and the country," his father said with authority.

"I understand," responded Donald.

At 7:30 in the dark of night, the ship on the river above the British camp suddenly swung open the side ports, and the pirates opened fire on the unsuspecting redcoats. The cannons roared. The artillery cut loose with grapeshot, killing and wounding a number British soldiers and causing others to panic.

When the cannons stopped firing, a flare was shot in the air from the ship, a signal to the local units to advance on the British. About a thousand swept down in the darkness into the camp, shooting and stabbing the surprised British with much hand-to-hand fighting.

Donald and his father fought side by side for a while but in the darkness and the fog of the night, became separated.

Donald saw the enemy firsthand and at close range. The British soldiers were fighting with rifles, knives, and swords after recovering from the surprise attack by the Americans.

Donald was shooting and reloading his rifle as fast as he could when he was hit with a bullet in the shoulder, knocking him to the ground. "Ahh!" he yelled. It hurt like hell. After a moment he jumped to his feet. His fear of dying kept him at the task of reloading his rifle.

Suddenly, he came face-to-face with a British soldier. He grabbed the end of the redcoat's rifle to prevent himself from being shot and instinctively pulled his knife from his belt with his other hand and stabbed his attacker in the stomach.

He watched in horror as the surprised British soldier sank to his knees in agony from the knife wound, and then keeled over dead. This was the first time Donald actually knew he killed someone. He was half in shock. With his eyes and mouth wide open, he stared at the lifeless man.

But the fighting around him quickly brought him back to his senses. His heart was pounding. In spite of the coolness of the evening, he could feel the sweat on his brow, and he made sure he joined with other Americans.

It was important they attack as a group and he not be separated from the rest, which might lead to a certain death. The fighting went on for several hours in the dead of night.

Donald, though wounded in the shoulder, was finally able to get back to the American lines with the help from others. It was only then that he learned his father had been killed. He became extremely emotional, and for the first time in many years, he began to sob.

Some of the men in his group tried to console him, and one of them helped him get to the medical site to treat his shoulder. Julie's father finally got around to bandaging Donald's wound after treating some of the other more seriously wounded men.

Around 10 o'clock, a thousand-man regiment of British Highlanders arrived from the ships to support those fighting the Americans, and the battle began to change in their favor. Jackson ordered a retreat about midnight.

The British, though, had suffered a bloody nose and a black eye in the skirmish. All told, the British suffered casualties to 276 officers and men, with forty-six killed. The Americans had 213 casualties, with only twenty-four dead.

CHAPTER THIRTEEN

Back in town the temporary hospitals were ready for the wounded. Julie helped get beds and bandages ready for the expected casualties. She noticed the Ursuline nuns and how efficiently they moved about preparing for the worst in their starched habits. They all could hear the distant roar of cannons, and they knew the battle had begun.

Later that night, the injured began to arrive. Julie was shocked when she saw Donald come in with a bloody shoulder. The injury was serious, and he lost a lot of blood, but the wound was not fatal.

He was totally despondent at the loss of his father. "My father is dead," sobbed Donald as he tried to control his emotions.

Julie tried to calm him while replacing his bloody bandage. "I'm so sorry," she said. Donald's thoughts about what happened that night swirled in his head.

As time went on that evening, Julie helped her father treat other men but often returned to give special attention to Donald. Later that night, although very weak from the loss of blood, Julie helped Donald walk out of the hospital and back home to his mother.

Agatha shrieked with horror and collapsed in tears when she learned her husband had been killed. This time it was Donald who did the consoling. "He was fighting for you, Mother. He didn't want the British to cause you harm." Donald continued to give solace to his mother while attempting to control his own emotions.

Julie did the best she could at giving comfort to the two. After a while she went back to the makeshift hospital to help her dad.

During the days of ensuing battles, many men were brought into the temporary hospitals, some with minor injuries but others with serious wounds. A few died after a short stay. Julie's father showed her how to treat and bandage the injuries. It was the first time she saw naked men being prepped for surgery.

At times she felt sick at seeing some of the horrible injuries the men had suffered. Some had arms shot off, and others had to have legs amputated. After a while, it became routine, and she was able to erase the emotions she felt and concentrate on helping her father treat the men with their injuries.

CHAPTER FOURTEEN

After several days and a number of skirmishes, the final assault by the British came on January 8th. By this time they had amassed more than five thousand men from the ships. But the plan of attack was flawed and not followed by some of the redcoat units. They were either delayed in their mission or did not properly understand or follow orders.

Ramon had been excited to be a part of fighting the enemy. His excitement turned to fear when the British charged the rampart on that final day of battle. Using his own rifle, he fired at the advancing enemy as fast as he could.

A number of British troops got close enough to cross the creek in front of the rampart and climb up the steep bank of the defensive mound. Most were cut down by the cannons and riflemen behind the earthen bank. But two officers did manage to reach the top.

One was fatally shot. The other taken prisoner. After seeing their officers killed and captured, the redcoats suddenly turned and ran. Some of them were shot and killed. Many were injured.

After a while, the remaining British troops were able to retreat to their camp out of range of the bullets and cannon balls. It was then the boom of the cannons and the crack of the rifles began to subside.

When the firing ceased, Ramon was shocked at the sight of all the dead men in the field in front of him, and he felt sick in the stomach. He tried to throw up, but it amounted to only dry heaves.

A Baratarian pirate saw Ramon's dismay and, clapping him hard on the back, said, "It's better them than you! The British are the ones who invaded the country. It's their fault they're dead."

Ramon could only weakly shake his head in agreement. "You're right," he said.

The next day, the British sent a message to Jackson asking for a temporary truce so the two sides could bury the dead. Most of those killed were Englishmen. Over eight hundred of the redcoats had died. Few Americans lost their lives in the last battle, about fifty-five.

Work details from both sides met in the center of the field with the British, collecting the dead and digging a large mass grave to bury their fallen comrades.

Ramon was part of the American detail to help collect the bodies. Not in his worst imagination could he believe the ghastly scene before him. The stench of the dead was rising, with the faces of some of the dead bodies frozen in agony. "How terrible," thought Ramon, "that such a thing could happen, and how horrible war is." The images would haunt him for years to come.

Two of the British generals had been killed in the attack. That left Major General John Lambert in command.

That night, Lambert called a counsel of officers to decide their next move. They decided the fight was not worth the loss of men and realized they were at a disadvantage with the location they were in. They also erroneously assumed the "American army is three times our number," said one of the officers.

After hearing all the opinions of his officers, and the disastrous defeat and the huge loss of men, Lambert decided it was time to retreat back to the ships.

With campfires burning that night to give a sense of normalcy, and fake sentries guarding the camp, the English stole away into the darkness.

CHAPTER FIFTEEN

It was not until the next morning that General Jackson realized the British were gone. From atop his horse, Jackson declared, "Gentlemen, we have won the battle." A roar of cheers went up from the men who had been defending the rampart, and there was much celebration that they had defeated the English.

Ramon and his father hugged each other and jumped for joy. "We won," said a jubilant Ramon.

The news that the invading army had fled quickly began to circulate throughout New Orleans. Many people began celebrating in the streets. Huge sighs of relief were seen on the faces of many people. Shouts of happiness were heard everywhere.

Julie's dad, who had worked many hours without sleep taking care of the wounded, hugged his daughter. "I thank God that we are safe," he said. "I am so happy the British have been defeated."

Julie cried tears of joy, partly due to the exhaustion she felt helping her father for many hours on end, but also the feeling of relief so many felt that New Orleans would not suffer from the invading redcoats.

Then Julie began to think about Donald, who she hadn't seen in several days. "Donald," she exclaimed, "I wonder how he is and if he has heard the good news." She scrambled out the door and hastened to his house to tell him.

Donald was sitting in a chair when Julie burst through the door and excitedly told him, "The British have left! They are going back to their ships!"

They embraced in happiness. Except Donald groaned in pain because Julie had wrapped her arms around his wounded shoulder and squeezed with joy.

Realizing that Donald was in pain, she let go. "Oh, I'm so sorry," she said. But Donald assured her, "It's all right. It was a happy pain."

It was the first good news Donald had since his father was killed. His despondency seemed to ease with the revelation that the fight was over.

With the threat gone, Donald began to think about the future. "Without father, my mother and I will have to run the business," he said.

He was about to turn eighteen in a few days. All of a sudden, the future looked a little bit brighter. Especially with Julie at his side, Donald could see his life becoming much happier. "What a wonderful day this is," he said. With that thought in mind, he pulled Julie close to him and gently kissed her on the lips.

At first, Julie was surprised, and her eyes opened wide as he pressed his lips to hers. But she quickly felt the warmth of his feelings toward her and returned the emotion she felt from Donald.

It was a moment of bliss neither had ever felt before. The pain from the wound in his shoulder seemed to suddenly disappear.

Donald's mother walked in the room about that time and saw the hug and kiss and the tenderness that Julie exhibited with her son. Her feelings toward Julie began to soften.

After she heard the good news about the British., "Oh, thank God," she said. Then, looking very pleasantly at Julie, she said, "Would you like something to drink?"

At first Julie was surprised by Agatha's presence, but noticing a different attitude toward her, said "Why yes, thank you for the offer."

34

CHAPTER SIXTEEN

Outside, the town was in a celebration. The mayor and the town council decided they would hold a parade and a dance at the French consulate. This would be attended by prominent citizens of the town, along with General Jackson and his officers. Also in attendance would be Jean Lafitte and his brothers Pierre and Dominic.

The night of the celebration was a huge gathering of towns people. A local band played waltzes and polkas. Then the mayor gave a speech in the middle of the event. "I want to thank all of the men and women who helped in the defense of the city," he said. "I compliment all the troops for defeating the British: the army, those from Tennessee and Alabama, all the volunteers, and Lafitte's men."

The celebration went on for hours. Lafitte's brothers left early, but Jean stayed and danced several times with some local prominent women. Many in the crowd gossiped about this mysterious, handsome, and well-dressed man believed to be a pirate.

Before he left, he shook hands with a number of important people and others he had never met before. This included

Ramon and his father, which he recognized as being with his men on the defensive line.

"I thank you for your efforts," he told Ramon and his father. "If you ever needed a job," he told Ramon, "you are welcome to join my organization."

Ramon's father did not like the offer to his son. He grimaced and shook his head no behind Lafitte's back, for he hoped that Ramon would eventually take over the blacksmith shop. But he restrained his feelings, for he did not want to offend the man who had given him so much business.

Ramon, on the other hand, was delighted to hear that a man such as Jean Lafitte would offer him an opportunity to do something that was more than working in a blacksmith shop. Here was a chance to see something more than New Orleans. "Thank you, sir. I may take you up on that." Much to his father's chagrin. "I welcome the opportunity," Ramon said.

As pillars of the community, Donald and his mother attended the event, as did Dr. Finch and Julie. As expected, Julie and Donald gravitated toward each other, enjoying several dances together. Dr. Finch and Mrs. Borden were both pleased to see their offspring hit it off at the event.

"They are a handsome couple," gushed Mrs. Borden. Dr. Finch could only nod his head in agreement.

Agatha had begun to realize the future with her husband gone. Maybe it was time for Donald to marry and begin a family.

As midnight neared, Donald suggested, "Why don't we go outside and cool off a bit. It's awfully hot in here with all the people."

When they were alone outside, Donald turned serious. "I really like you. You are so beautiful. I could live with you the rest of my life."

"Oh?" responded Julie, a little shocked and surprised at his words. When she recovered her composure, she responded, "Well, I really like you too."

That was enough for Donald. He reached in his pocket and pulled out a small box which he opened, containing a beautiful but small diamond ring. He knelt down on his knee and, with much emotion in his voice, said, "Will you marry me?"

At first Julie gasped. "Oh my God," she said, her eyes wide open and looking at the ring. Then looking into the eager eyes of Donald, realizing this was to be her future, blurted out, "Yes!"

Then the two kissed and embraced, their hearts pounding with excitement. "I will cherish you the rest of my life," said Donald.

"And I you," responded Julie.

After holding each other for a moment, Julie's head suddenly shot back and shut her eyes tight. "What's the matter?" asked Donald.

Then, collecting her thoughts on what just happened, she said, "I hope my father approves."

"I hope so too," responded Donald.

They lingered awhile on the patio, smiling and holding hands. Then they returned to the ballroom to inform their parents about their decision to get married.

In a very formal way, Donald screwed up his courage and said, "Dr. Finch, I really like Julie. As a matter of fact, I love her. I have asked for her hand in marriage, and she has agreed. Will you give us your blessing?"

At first, Julie's father was a little taken aback by the decision of his daughter. Yes, she was about to turn seventeen, but was she ready for marriage?

"Well," he said very slowly and with a very serious look his face. "Aren't you a little young for marriage?"

"I'm almost seventeen, Father. And I think I understand what marriage is about," she replied.

Donald's mother spoke up then and, turning to Julie's father, said, "I think your daughter is mature enough to handle marriage with our help. Donald is almost eighteen, and I think he would make a very stable husband."

In the back of her mind, she hoped he was about to settle down with a wife and help run the family business.

Dr. Finch realized he was outnumbered and didn't want to argue the point in public. "I will give you my consent," he said. "But I suggest you set the time for a wedding sometime in March when the weather would be better and you are a little bit older. That way you both will be sure this is really what you want to do," he said.

That brought big smiles to the couple's faces, and they agreed that would be a good idea.

It was then Julie gave her father a big hug and then a hug for Mrs. Borden. Donald shook his soon to be father-in-law's hand vigorously. "Thank you, sir. Thank you very much," Everyone was smiling and very happy with the night's event.

CHAPTER SEVENTEEN

For Ramon, the end of the battle was the beginning of a new life for him. He began to make friends with some of the nicer men of Lafitte's group. "Why don't you join Lafitte's outfit," they said. "You might see something more than New Orleans."

This excited Ramon. "Yeah, I think I will," he said.

The next time he saw his friend Donald, he told him his plans to join Lafitte's organization. "Isn't that a little dangerous?" asked Donald.

"Nah," said Ramon. "Besides, I've been told I could become a very rich man."

Jean Lafitte, on the other hand, was disappointed about the governor's continued bad feeling toward him. When he was arrested before the British came, the local government had confiscated his ships and all his merchandise the local law enforcement could find on Barataria.

Since the government would not allow him to personally get his ships back, he paid a close local friend who was eligible to buy the ships for Lafitte. He then collected as many men as he could, rounded up all his hidden goods, and sailed from Barataria to an island in the south of Texas, which is now known as Galveston. He called it Campeche.

Ramon heard about Lafitte's plan to leave. He decided that his future was elsewhere, much to the dismay of his father. This resulted in a heated argument with his father. "I adamantly refuse to give to you permission to leave New Orleans."

But the day Lafitte was leaving Barataria for Campeche, Ramon snuck out of the house and made his way to join Lafitte and his crew.

After a two-day sail, Lafitte's ship arrived at Campeche, much to Ramon's disappointment. Campeche was on a barren island with few trees, bushes, some grass, and a few rattlesnakes. Not to mention a band of hostile Indians who lived on the mainland but did not like the invasion of the white men in their territory.

Ramon was put to work helping to build a fairly nice house for Lafitte and his mistress, and a number of shacks for himself and Lafitte's men.

For the next few weeks, pirate ships would anchor on the ocean side of the island. Because of the shallower waters, they would bring in merchandise on smaller boats to the inland side. Lafitte would buy the goods at half price or less. Ramon was assigned to help other men store the merchandise in a large warehouse.

When the warehouse was full, Lafitte sent word to merchants in New Orleans to meet him halfway to Campeche to purchase the goods.

Lafitte told Ramon to go with the men and help pull the wagons and carts full of captured merchandise. Armed men would also accompany the group to protect it from hostile Indians.

It had been more than a month since Ramon had joined the Lafitte band, and the work was getting rather tedious. He had hoped to be on a sailing ship. He began to long for the city life and his father's blacksmith shop. Most of the men he was with at Campeche were older than he, and he didn't quite seem to fit in.

This made Ramon a little homesick. He missed his father and his friends, particularly Donald and Julie. He had hoped he would have more experience on a sailing ship. None of that came true.

Then an event happened that changed his life for ever. A pirate ship came to Lafitte's hideout loaded with goods to sell. The captain of the ship came ashore and was greeted by Lafitte, who was anxious to buy the merchandise.

With the captain was a young girl who had serious head injuries. She had two black eyes, a split lip, and a swollen face with bruises from being hit with a fist. She had blood stains on her blouse.

"What's with her?" asked Lafitte.

"Well," said the captain, "she got mixed up with a crew member who was trying to seduce her when no one was looking. She started screaming at the top of her lungs, and he started hitting her on the head to make her shut up. The screaming brought the first mate, who pulled him off her just in time and clacked him in irons for damaging the goods. She's only fifteen, but with a battered face like that, who's going to want her? I was going to offer her to a madam in Guatemala. But, I'll sell her to you for one hundred dollars. You can use her as a servant or whatever."

"Where did you get her?" asked Lafitte.

"I got her off a ship I captured. One hundred dollars and she's yours."

Lafitte was about to answer when a voice behind him said boldly, "I'll give you fifty dollars."

Startled, Lafitte slowly turned around only to see Ramon standing there with fifty dollars in his fist.

"Are you sure you want this poor little wretch?" asked Lafitte.

"Yes," said Ramon. "Who would treat a young girl like that?" Ramon's sympathetic face let Lafitte know Ramon was serious about helping the poor girl.

"I tell you what," said Lafitte turning back to the captain. "We'll give you seventy-five dollars and some good deals on the merchandise you want to sell."

The captain's face turned grim for a moment, looking first at Ramon and then at Lafitte. Then his face turned from grim into a serious smile. "OK," said the pirate. "You got a deal." With that he shoved the young girl at Ramon.

At first, the girl's arms were crossed and her head down. Ramon tried to take her hand, but she refused. "I won't hurt you. I promise," said Ramon in a sympathetic tone. She looked at him in a stare of disbelief. And again she refused his hand. With that, Ramon put his hand behind her back and gently pushed her away from the encounter.

Realizing this might be better than going back to the ship, she reluctantly let Ramon lead her away from the pirate captain. But before they could get far, Lafitte told Ramon, "Take her to my house and let my woman look after her."

When they reached the house, Dotty, a middle-aged woman of mixed race, came outside and immediately saw how seriously the girl had been hurt and pulled the girl toward her. "You stay outside," said Dotty sternly to Ramon. "I take care of her." She then grabbed the girl by the arm and hustled her inside.

About an hour later, Dotty and the girl emerged from the house. She had been cleaned up, her hair was combed, and she was wearing a nice clean dress that was too large for her small frame. "What you gonna do with her?" Dotty demanded.

"Nothing," responded Ramon. "I just felt sorry for her."

"She no woman yet! You be nice to her," she said in a stern voice.

"I will," responded Ramon. "I will not hurt her."

With that Dotty let go of the girl, crossed her arms, and watched as the two walked away. The girl hoped Ramon was telling the truth, and the trauma she suffered on the ship would not be repeated.

CHAPTER EIGHTEEN

When they got to his shack, he offered her some food, to which she nodded her head yes. She hadn't eaten in two days. He gave her a banana, which she anxiously devoured. Ramon fixed some bacon and cornbread on a wood stove that was still hot from the morning breakfast.

At first, their relationship was strained. Ramon asked her what her name was. She refused to answer. "OK," said Ramon, "I'll call you Sandy."

"My name not Sandy!" the girl suddenly and emphatically responded, speaking for the first time with a slightly French accent.

When Ramon tried to touch her, Sandy would withdraw. "I am not a whore," said the girl vehemently.

"I know," responded Ramon. "I promise, I will not hurt you."

That night, he gave her the only bed in the shack, while he slept on a mat on the floor. The next morning, after a long night went by with difficulty sleeping on the hard surface, Ramon complained he had enough of sleeping on the mat.

"Tonight," he said, "I'm going to join you on the bed. I promise, I will not molest you."

She gave him a stern look. "OK," she said with conviction. "But we will have separate blankets. You will not touch me. And we will get another bed as soon as possible."

Smiling, Ramon agreed. He was so relieved to get off the floor, and to be close to her would be wonderful.

The next day was stressful for both of them. Ramon still had questions. "Where did you come from? How did you wind up on a pirate ship? And where are your parents?" he asked.

"My parents are gone," she replied sadly. "My father was killed when the pirates attacked the ship. My mother was sent with the other ship to a port I know not where."

"I'm very sorry," said Ramon as he put his arm around her shoulder. And for the first time, she did not pull back.

Days went by and Ramon and Sandy began to relate to each other. Sandy's emotional guard began to relax, and she realized that Ramon wanted to be her friend. She began to cook his meals and clean the cabin.

Her swollen face began to get better, and Ramon could see she was a beautiful young woman. Her dark brown hair and slim figure was hard not to notice.

One night after dinner, Ramon kissed her gently on the forehead. She froze, thinking she was about to be assaulted. Ramon saw how uneasy she was and backed off.

"It's OK," he said, gently patting her on the shoulder, to which she began to relax.

"OK," she said quietly. After all, Ramon had been treating her very good since she got off the ship.

"I appreciate that you have been nice to me," she said. "I hope that continues."

"It will," Ramon assured her.

Still, her sad face remained, never smiling, always grim. Ramon tried to cheer her up but to no avail.

The next day, with Ramon away with work, Sandy decided it was time to try and clean herself. She hadn't had a bath in days, and she occasionally used a wet wash cloth to get the dirt and sweat off her body.

Standing in a large but shallow metal pan, Sandy poured water from a pitcher over her head and naked body. It felt so good to be clean again.

She had just about finished when Ramon suddenly walked through the door. "Aaahhh!" screamed Sandy as she scrambled to grab a towel and cover her body from her neck down to just above her knees. "Get out!" she yelled. And visions of being attacked again like on the pirate ship ran through her head.

Ramon was dumbfounded. He had seen for a brief moment a beautiful young woman totally naked, and now only partially covered by a towel.

"Get out!" Sandy angrily repeated to a now gently smiling Ramon.

He then responded in a soft and gentle tone, "You are very beautiful."

The remark startled Sandy. Was this complement a prelude to being attacked again? She tried a different tact. Echoing Ramon's softer tone, but deliberately emphasizing and pausing in between each word, Sandy said, "Please…Leave…Now!"

Still gently smiling, Ramon nodded his head and began to slowly back up to the door, still looking at Sandy. He reached for the doorknob behind his back, slowly opened the door, and backed out. Still smiling and looking at Sandy, he slowly closed the door and walked away.

Sandy, breathing heavily, paused for a second, thinking he might return.

When nothing happened, she tossed the towel and quickly got dressed, even though her body was still wet from the makeshift shower.

Ramon, still smiling, returned to the warehouse. One of the pirates, who had been rearranging the captured merchandise, said tersely "What are you smiling about?" Ramon did not respond, only picking up some of the material and moving it about.

When Ramon returned to the shed that night, he knocked on the door to warn Sandy he was coming in. To his surprise she had fixed a dinner of pasta, with some peaches she had obtained from Dotty.

Neither said a word. Sandy did not look at Ramon. They both sat down to the dinner and ate in silence.

After dinner, as Sandy was putting the dirty dishes in a bucket she used as a wash pan, Ramon finally spoke. "I'm sorry about today," he said in an apologetic tone, although he really didn't mean it.

After a long moment, and not turning to face Ramon, Sandy tersely responded, "Apology accepted."

CHAPTER NINETEEN

As days went by, Ramon got tired of hauling material around the camp brought in by pirates. He finally told Sandy, "You know, it sure would be nice to be back in New Orleans at my father's blacksmith shop. Besides, you need to be in a more civilized environment."

Ramon had begun to notice that some of the men in camp were beginning to admire the beautiful young woman whose head injuries had almost completely healed.

She also felt uncomfortable with the stares she received from some of the men when she walked to Dotty's house for conversation and to get things she needed for the shack.

Ramon suggested, "The next time Lafitte has enough merchandise to trade with merchants, we should leave. We could travel with the caravan, and instead of coming back to Campeche, go on to New Orleans."

Sandy whole heartedly agreed with that idea. "Oh yes," she said. She was no longer afraid of Ramon and did not like the primitive shack she was living in or the stares she got from some of the men. "I will be more than happy to get back to civilization."

Besides, the U.S. government was threatening to kick Lafitte and his men off the Texas island. They gave him a month to destroy his camp and leave Campeche.

The trip the two teenagers took with other men half way to New Orleans to meet the merchants went without a hitch. And who was among the merchants buying goods? None other than Donald, who had taken over his father's business and was running the store along with his mother.

"How are you?" asked Donald of Ramon as the two embraced as long-lost friends. They were both happy to see each other. "It's so good to see you again. Been on any pirate ships?" asked Donald.

"No, not really," answered Ramon. "How is my father?"

"Oh, he's fine," answered Donald. "He's still mad at you for leaving New Orleans, but he's also sad you are not there any more."

Then Ramon introduced Sandy to his friend, and Donald's eyes widened. He was surprised at the age and beauty of the young woman.

Ramon explained the situation. "She was taken off a ship that was captured by pirates. One of the pirates beat her up."

"Please to meet you," said Donald.

"Thank you," she said politely.

The rest of the trip back to New Orleans went off without a problem.

And when Ramon arrived at the home of his father, there was a great celebration. They embraced several times. "How happy I am to see you alive and well," said the father. The old anger he felt when Ramon left town was gone.

"I'm happy to be home," admitted Ramon.

At first, the father was not sure about the young girl with Ramon. "And who is this?" he asked.

After Ramon explained what happened to her, his father opened his arms and welcomed her to New Orleans. "My home is your home. You can stay as long as you like," said the father.

And for the first time, a smile came across Sandy's face. She felt the genuine warmth of Ramon's father and was very happy with her new surroundings. Then she turned to Ramon and gave him a big smile and a long hug.

That night there was a big celebration. The whole neighborhood joined in the party along with Julie, her father, and Donald and his mother. There was a big platter of shrimp, barbecued chicken, fruit, and vegetables. A quartet of local musicians played, and people danced and sang.

Ramon's father topped the celebration with a toast. Raising his glass, he said, "To my son, and to his beautiful companion, I hope for them a beautiful and wonderful long life."

"Here, here!" everybody joined in. And the party continued well into the night.

It was a celebration that many remembered for years to come.

CHAPTER TWENTY

As time went on, Sandy became the woman of the house, cleaning, cooking, and taking care of the two older men. Ramon and Sandy also became much closer as a couple. She turned sixteen years old about the time that Ramon became eighteen. She also became more affectionate to Ramon, allowing him to kiss her, but nothing else.

He learned his lesson. One time after a nice kiss, he put his hand on her rear. The immediate reaction was a sudden push by Sandy and stern rebuke of "no, no!"

To which Ramon, with a broad grin on his face and putting his hands in the air as if surrendering, said, "OK." Sandy then gave him a glare to show that she meant what she said. And then it was over.

The two of them also became close friends to Julie and Donald. They would often do things together. Some days, when Donald and Ramon were at work, Julie and Sandy would go shopping together in town.

Julie understood the trauma that Sandy had undergone and did her best to make the younger woman feel comfortable.

Julie had turned seventeen and viewed Sandy more like a young sister.

Julie and Donald had finally set the date for their wedding. There was much excitement among family and friends.

About two weeks before the big event, when the two young couples were together, Julie had a sudden idea. She liked Sandy and Ramon. "You know," said Julie, "Donald and I are getting married soon. Why don't you and sandy get married with us? We'll make it a double wedding."

Sandy's mouth opened in wide astonishment. Ramon's eyebrows raised. Stunned at the suggestion, Sandy and Ramon looked at each other. Then Sandy began to have a smile on her face. The change of expression led Ramon to believe that this might be acceptable to Sandy.

"I would love to have you for a wife," said Ramon. Sandy's smile grew even bigger, and she gently nodded her head, which to Ramon meant this was a yes. This led to a long and passionate kiss. All of a sudden, the two couples were hugging each other, jumping up and down, and shouting with joy.

And so it came to pass. The two pairs were married the same day in the local church, with huge crowds attending. The Battle of New Orleans had brought the many different nationalities together. Here was a wedding with the daughter of an American, marrying a Scottish businessman, and a Creole marrying a young woman from France.

But that is not quite the end of the story. Donald expanded his father's business and became a very rich man. He also became a senator when Louisiana became a state of the union.

After raising five kids, Julie became a teacher and finally a superintendent of the school district. Her dedication increased the quality of education for all the students in New Orleans.

Ramon also had a successful life. After his father died, Ramon took over the blacksmith shop and added a livery stable with enough horses to satisfy the needs of the community.

But it was Sandy who ran the business. Her education before coming to America gave her the knowledge to make Ramon and her very successful business owners.

And what about the two most important men of the time? General Jackson ran for Congress and eventually became president of the United States.

And Lafitte? He left his colony on Campeche under threat of eviction by the U.S. government. He became a pirate, plundering ships from various countries, until he suddenly disappeared.

There were stories that he was mortally wounded in a battle with an English ship. Then there were other stories that he retired in St. Louis, Missouri, with his mistress and died a very old and rich man after living off merchandise he had stored away in an earlier life.

No one really knows for sure.

And the two couples? They lived happily ever after, with their children all becoming friends with one another. They kept alive the success of their parents, and contributed to the future of their state and nation.

Milton Keynes UK
Ingram Content Group UK Ltd.
UKHW020941220424
441551UK00019B/1488